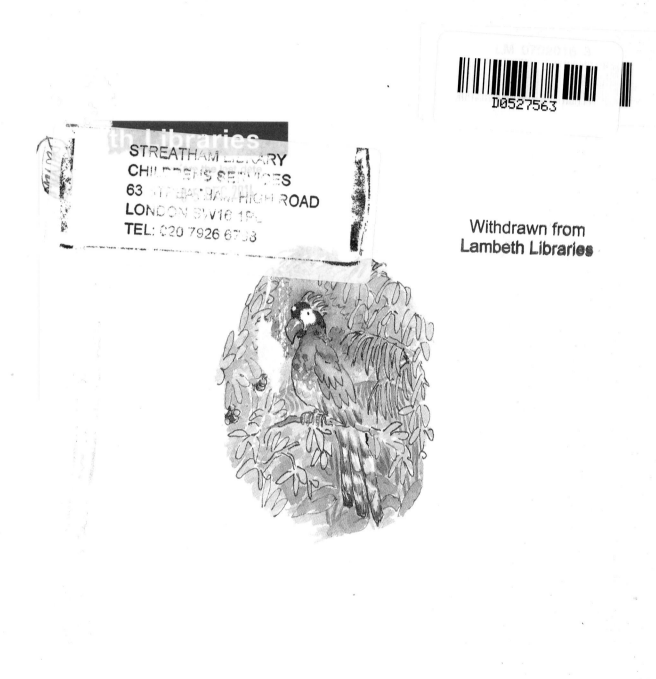

for Leo

First published in Great Britain by
HarperCollins Publishers Ltd in 1994
10 9 8 7 6 5 4 3 2 1
First published in Picture Lions in 1994
10 9 8 7 6 5 4 3 2 1
Picture Lions is an imprint of the Children's Division,
part of HarperCollins Publishers Limited,
77-85 Fulham Palace Road, Hammersmith,
London W6 8JB
ISBN 0 00 193992 0 (Hardback)
ISBN 0 00 664419 8 (Picture Lions)
Text and illustrations copyright © Rachel Pank 1994
The author asserts the moral right to be identified as the author of this work.
A CIP catalogue record for this title is available from the British Library.
Produced by HarperCollins Hong Kong
This book is set in 20/26 cochin

LEO
and the
Wallpaper Jungle

Rachel Pank

Collins
An Imprint of HarperCollinsPublishers

Leo was not
a tiny baby
any more.

Although next to
Big People, he
looked very small.

Leo's Mum and Dad had finished decorating his own room. It had very special wallpaper.

Mum and Dad thought the room was lovely.
Leo was not sure.

Leo was to sleep in his new bedroom for the first time. The wallpaper was full of jungle animals, but no one had noticed that there was no lion. The King of the Jungle was missing.

It was time for bed. Dad tucked Leo up and kissed him. "Night night."

Leo looked at the
jungle around him.

It grew darker.
Leo sucked his toes.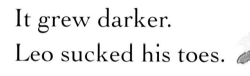

He rolled over.

 He turned around.

Leo was not sure.

As the night grew quiet and still
Leo heard a rustling sound.
He stared at the new wallpaper.
And, as the room grew darker and darker,
the animals stared back...

"He's stripey like me,"
said Tiger.

"He's called Leo," Monkey
said and he swung through
the trees to get a closer look.

"He's very small," said
Elephant, in a big voice.

"Leo is the name of the King
of the Jungle," said Parrot,
who knew everything.

Parrot and the other birds carried the word quickly through the trees. Soon a crowd began to gather as the animals moved nearer to catch a glimpse of the King of the Jungle.

"Surely the King of the Jungle is
supposed to be a fearsome beast?"
said Tiger.
Other voices rose up in the crowd.
The animals were confused, Leo was
not at all what they had expected.

Poor Leo was not happy with his new room. He could not see Mum and Dad's bed and all the animals in the wallpaper were whispering about him.

"He doesn't look big and brave enough to be a King,"
said Giraffe. "He doesn't look like he could stand
up for himself, or anyone else," said Monkey.
"We need a proper Leo round here!"
boomed Elephant. "A proper lion,"
squawked Parrot. "One that roars,"
growled Tiger.

Leo began to sniffle and snuffle.
Where was Dad? Where was Mum?

The animals were not happy either.
"He can't stay here," said Elephant.
"We need a proper King, a proper
roaring Leo the Lion!"

Leo began to cry but no one could
hear him. So he opened his mouth
for his very loudest cry...

...and out of his mouth

came

a

HUGE

ROAR

With that the animals dashed behind the trees in fright. Mum rushed in and picked Leo up. She didn't notice that all the animals were hiding.

After a nice long cuddle and a kiss, Leo was sleepy and didn't mind going back into his cot.

As Mum tiptoed out, one by one the animals shyly peeped out from behind the trees.

The animals did not know what to do.
"Your Majesty!" said Monkey. "You
are a real King... may I offer you
a banana?"

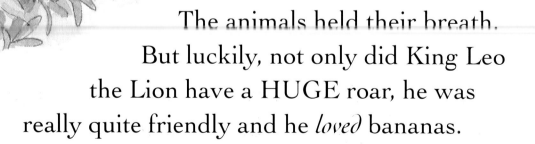

The animals held their breath.
But luckily, not only did King Leo
the Lion have a HUGE roar, he was
really quite friendly and he *loved* bananas.

From that night on, to Mum and Dad's surprise,
Leo went happily to bed in his new room.

Of course, they didn't know that
he was in his own secret Kingdom,
for Leo *was* the King of the Jungle!